"When I was a boy and I would see scary things in the news, my mother would say to me,
'Look for the helpers. You will always find people who are helping."
-Mr. Rogers

To all of the helpers . . .
-C.M.

and to Hercules,
the noblest dog I know.
-N.H.

Reedy Press
PO Box 5131
St. Louis, MO 63139
www.reedypress.com

PAWS K-9 Search and Rescue: www.peopleareworthsaving.org
Carolyn Mueller: www.carolynelizabethmueller.com
Lily's Page: www.facebook.com/k9lily

Library of Congress Control Number: 2014931427
ISBN: 978-1-935806-67-7

Printed in the United States of America
14 15 16 17 18   1 2 3 4 5

lily

a true story of courage & the Joplin Tornado

written by
Carolyn E Mueller

illustrated by
Nick Hayes

REEDY PRESS

St. Louis, Missouri

This is Lily.

This is Tara.

They live here. In Joplin, Missouri.

Tara found Lily when she was a tiny puppy.

But Lily wasn't so small for long! She had big paws!

And BIG energy!

Tara knew just what to do with her crazy Weimaraner. Lily needed a job!

And so Tara trained Lily to become a search and rescue dog.

They started out easy, playing hide and seek with Tara's children in the backyard.

Lily **ALWAYS** won!

One night, an elderly woman wandered into the dark, dark woods.

Police called Lily and Tara to the scene.

Lily picked up the woman's scent and followed it into the forest where she saved the old lady's life!

Lily had proven herself as a real search and rescue dog! She helped whenever she was called.

One day Lily, herself, needed help. She became very sick. Tara thought that she was going to lose her best friend.

The veterinarians decided to give Lily a special medicine.

And do you know what?

It worked!

Lily was going to be OK!
It was a miracle, but
Lily's challenges were
far from over...

One month later,
something bad happened.

Something very, very bad.

A terrible storm hit
Joplin, Missouri.

This swirling, whirling beast tore straight through the middle of Joplin!

Many people were hurt, missing, or lost.

Lily had a job to do!

She went out into the ruined streets searching for people who needed help.

As they searched, Lily got glass in her paws. Tara found a nail stuck in her boot. It was hot. It was rainy. And sometimes it even continued to lightning and thunder.

But they found and helped people who had been hurt by the storm.

Tara and Lily were asked to search the local hospital. The tornado had walloped St. John's, and Lily had to make sure that no one was inside the damaged building.

Tara, though, was afraid of heights. She was nervous about searching the hospital because she needed to go all the way up to the roof.

As Lily and Tara climbed the wobbly staircase, a group of firefighters circled around them to be sure that they were safe. Tara felt better with Lily at her side.

When they finally reached the top,
Tara was shocked by what she saw.

She saw that everything had changed.

But then she looked a little bit closer.

Down below, amidst the wreckage, she saw neighbors.
They were passing out water to people on the street!

Friends found each other,
only wanting to hug.

She saw a lone tree, hung with birdhouses so Joplin's birds could still have a place to call home...

Churches and stores opened their doors so that everyone who had lost so much could find shelter.

There were police officers and firefighters, soldiers and EMTs sorting through the rubble.

They worked side by side, putting the town back together slowly, piece by piece.

On the top of that hospital, Tara and Lily saw miles of destruction.

But they also saw helpers. They saw everyday heroes. They saw lots of friends.

In the evening, after a long day of searching, Tara took Lily home.

She sat on the porch as Lily ran out into the yard.

She watched as Lily rolled in the grass. That beautiful dog wagged her tail in the setting sun, as if nothing bad had ever happened.

Tara had almost lost Lily.

But Lily was going to be okay.

...Joplin would be okay too.

Meet the Real Lily and Tara

Lily the Weimaraner and Tara Prosser are a real-life search and rescue (SAR) team living and working in Joplin, Missouri. Tara has worked as both an EMT and a 911 dispatcher, and she has always had an interest in dog training. After bringing Lily home as a puppy, the two began their search and rescue adventure first through basic obedience classes and then through the training guidance of a local rescue team.

SAR dogs are canines trained for the purpose of helping others. They assist with missing persons, rescues, and disaster relief. These dogs use their phenomenal sense of smell to detect human scent. There are four main types of SAR dogs: air scenting, tracking, trailing, and cadaver dogs. Any dog can be trained to become a search and rescue dog. As a Weimaraner, Lily is a member of a sporting breed. These animals make great SAR dogs because they know how to work closely with humans.

Together, with local SAR enthusiasts, Tara founded PAWS K-9 Search and Rescue. The team is always on call and available to assist law enforcement with missing persons and rescues. Tara also works to educate the community about SAR dogs, making sure people are aware of when and how these amazing animals can be utilized. Tara, Lily, and the other PAWS members are volunteers who commit their time and talents for the purpose of helping others.

Tara lives with her husband, Jeff, their two children, Ivy and Jacob, and their dogs, Lily and Daisey, in Joplin.

About the Joplin Tornado

On the evening of May 22, 2011, a category F-5 tornado hit Joplin, Missouri. This storm was the deadliest tornado to hit the United States since 1947. It ripped straight through the center of Joplin with 200 mph winds. The tornado killed 158 people and injured another 1,000. Many more were left homeless or with damaged property. Emergency workers and citizens, such as Tara and Lily, banded together to assist with recovery efforts in Joplin.